To Naseer, Sujude, and Nuah. To all of our past,
present, and future halal food adventures.
—SA

To all the lovely children who love street food. ☺
—PS

 little bee books

New York, NY
Text copyright © 2021 by Susannah Aziz
Illustrations copyright © 2021 by Parwinder Singh
All rights reserved, including the right of reproduction
in whole or in part in any form.
Manufactured in China RRD 0121
littlebeebooks.com
First Edition
10 9 8 7 6 5 4 3 2 1
Library of Congress Cataloging-in-Publication Data
Names: Aziz, Susannah, author. | Singh, Parwinder, illustrator.
Title: Halal hot dogs / by Susannah Aziz; illustrated by Parwinder Singh.
Description: First edition. | New York, NY: Little Bee Books, 2021. | Audience: Ages 4-8. Audience:
Grades 2-3. | Summary: Every Friday, Musa's family takes turns picking out a Jummah treat which
they use to try all different foods, but when it is Musa's turn, he sticks to his favorite halal hot
dogs to share. | Identifiers: LCCN 2020047151 | Subjects: CYAC: Halal food—Fiction. | Muslims—
United States—Fiction. | Family life—Fiction. | Classification: LCC PZ7.1.A988 Hal 2021 | DDC
[E]—dc23 | LC record available at https://lccn.loc.gov/2020047151
ISBN 978-1-4998-1157-5
For information about special discounts on bulk purchases,
please contact Little Bee Books at sales@littlebeebooks.com.

T 129553

HALAL HOT DOGS

WRITTEN BY SUSANNAH AZIZ

ILLUSTRATED BY PARWINDER SINGH

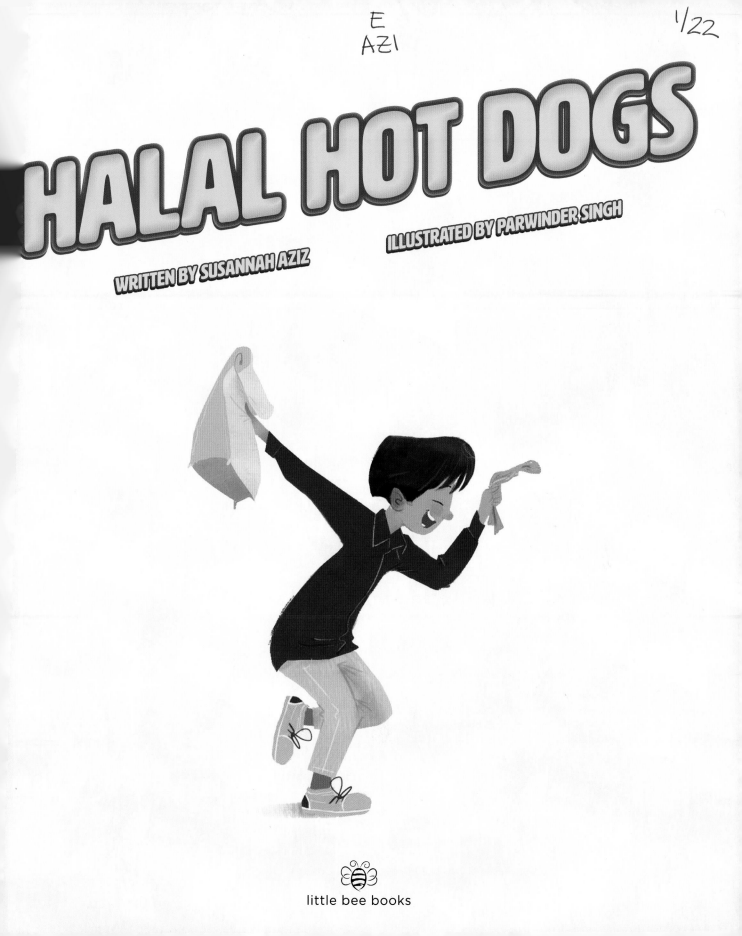

little bee books

Assalamu Alaikum!

My name is Musa

Ahmed

Abdul

Aziz

Moustafa

Abdel

Salam,

but most people just call me Musa.

Today is Friday, my favorite day of the week!
Every Friday, my family and I head to Jummah Prayer at the masjid.
Afterward, we go home and share a special Jummah treat.

But lately, our Jummah treats have been . . . interesting.

A couple of weeks ago, Mama made her molokhia.
It's great for slurping. And sharing!
But I accidentally squeezed lemon in Seedi's eye.
And we all had molokhia teeth for days.

The next week, Baba tried to grill some kufte kebabs.
We usually wrap them in pita bread with
pickled beets. They are pretty delicious!

They come out perfect when Mama makes them.
It turns out Baba's kufte was perfect . . . for playing soccer with.

Next, Seedi made his favorite, riz bi haleeb,
creamy rice pudding with yummy pistachio sprinkled on top.
But Seedi lost his teeth in the process.
We spent an hour searching the house.
Let's just say dentures aren't good for flavor.

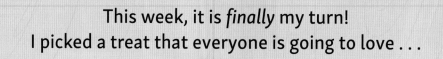

This week, it is *finally* my turn!
I picked a treat that everyone is going to love . . .

halal hot dogs!

I'm going to stop at the hot dog stand right after Jummah Prayer.
The one a block away from the masjid is the absolute *best*.
They make the halal hot dogs just right:

the perfect amount of hot,

chewy,

juicy,

hot dog goodness.

They also have a special sauce that we all love—Salam sauce!
Our family favorite, it's a perfect blend of white sauce and mustard.

We head out the door. I love walking to the masjid with my family. When we get really excited, we like to dance dabke. My baba taught me the steps.

begin to bend my knee and step,
bend my knee and step,
kick and STOMP!

I add my own jump at the end. It's really high.
I'm pretty sure I fly for four whole seconds!

I hear Seedi calling me back,
telling me to tie my shoes.
Sometimes I forget to do that.

When we finally arrive at the masjid,
we listen to the khutbah.
It's very long, and I am hungry.
My stomach rumbles and grumbles!

Imam Fawaz clears his throat
and gives me a side glance.

I try to focus during salat, like my baba and Seedi,
but my stomach ROARS away.

Louder.

And louder.

After salat, I'm ready in a flash with my shoes on!

It takes Seedi a while because he has to help Maryam find her red shoes.

Mama is catching up with friends.
I can't wait any longer!

My baba hands me some money and tells me to run ahead.
He's right behind me!

The different smells of the food stands are wonderful.
My mouth waters as I pass people eating . . .

falafel,

tacos,

bao,

shish kebab,

samosas,

churros,

fresh mango,

Italian ice, and . . .

I run into neighborhood friends buying halal hot dogs, too.
Liu Wei and Javier live on my block.

I guess my school principal,
Mrs. Iman, likes halal hot dogs, too.
She bought ten! I counted.

Fireman Rodriguez bought enough
for all the firefighters at the station!

Oh, no! What if they run out of halal hot dogs?
I hope there are some left for me!

We're all so excited for our Jummah treat!
But we made a rule: *No eating until we get home.*
I can't wait to share my treat!

I begin to . . .

bend my knee and step,

bend my knee and step,

kick and STOMP!

My jump must be the
highest ever recorded.
This time, I'm pretty sure
I flew for 8.654 seconds!

When I land, I'm home. *Finally.*
My family all gathers around.

I open the bag, reach in, and pull out . . .

They make halal hot dogs just right:

the perfect amount of hot,

chewy,

juicy,

hot dog goodness.

And they have special Salam sauce to dip them in.
The sauce tastes pretty good with falafel, too.

AUTHOR'S NOTE

This story was inspired by my son, Naseer, (Naseerasaurus Rex) and his love for halal hot dogs! As a Brooklyn kid, he enjoys exploring the many streets of our neighborhood along with his sister, Sujude (Judy), and his brother, Nuah (Nuah Bear), as they always stop at one of the many halal food carts on the way home from the many masjids. Though his love for halal hot dogs still remains, he has recently expanded his international food palette in creating his own signature recipes which include "mecluba sandwiches" and "the smash," which entails smashing two shawarma sandwiches together and then dousing them in green chiles, cheese, and "special sauce."

I want to thank my parents, Hannie and Nadia Aziz, for always supporting me. I love you so much! Baba, you are the dabke master! Mom, you're amazing! To my siblings: Alia, Iktimal, Sarah, Mohamed, and Farris, thank you for being my best friends. Thank you to the sweetest, most generous grandparents a girl could have: "Tata" Suaad and "Seedi" Wajeeh. Thank you to my husband for your support. Thank you to my large Palestinian family! Thank you to the best publishing agent in the world, Adria Goetz! Thank you, Courtney Fahy and to everyone at Little Bee Books, for wanting to share this story with the world.

A portion of the proceeds from this book will be donated to UNRWA USA—an American nonprofit committed to bettering the lives of Palestine refugees through advocacy efforts in the US and fundraising for UNRWA programs in the Middle East.

THE AUTHOR'S KIDDOS EATING HALAL HOT DOGS!

GLOSSARY OF ARABIC WORDS AND TERMS

Baba—Daddy
dabke—Middle Eastern dance
halal—permissible food according to Islamic religion
Imam—prayer leader of mosque
Jummah—congregational Friday prayer
khutbah—sermon
kufte—a type of grilled, spiced meatball made of chicken, beef, or lamb
masjid—mosque
mecluba—a Palestinian upside-down dish of meat, rice, and vegetables
molokhia—a thick, Middle Eastern stew made of green molokhia leaves and meat
riz bi haleeb—Middle Eastern rice pudding
salat—prayer
seedi—grandfather

HALAL LAWS

Halal is an Islamic term that refers to lawful, blessed, and permissible meat. There are guidelines to follow in order to ensure meat can be classified as halal, similar to Jewish kosher laws, but there are also differences between the two styles. It is preferable to eat halal meat in Muslim households, but there are exceptions if halal meat is not available. There are strict laws that prohibit eating pork or pork products, as well as carnivorous animals and birds of prey, among others. The animal from which the meat comes from must be healthy and have lived in ideal conditions. The animal cannot have been tortured, must have been fed a nutritious diet, and its killing must be done as quickly and humanely as possible. Rules are in place to enforce this. The meat must be blessed with a recitation from the Koran, which can be recited by anyone. In places such as large cities, halal restaurants and food stands—particularly halal hot dog stands—are widespread and prevalent. These food laws are adhered to in Muslim communities in order to achieve a healthy lifestyle in accordance with Islamic lifestyle.